KILL ORDER

DANIEL BLYTHE

Badger
LEARNING

Kill Order ISBN 978-1-78464-702-5

Text © Daniel Blythe 2017
Complete work © Badger Publishing Limited 2017

Publisher: Susan Ross
Senior Editor: Danny Pearson
Copyediting: Cambridge Publishing Management Ltd
Designer: Bigtop Design Ltd
Cover: I. Glory / Alamy

2 4 6 8 10 9 7 5 3 1

CHAPTER 1
ARRIVAL

Caleb had a kill mission waiting.

Still aching from the shuttle journey, he took his place in line at immigration control. He was a lean, tanned young man of 19, with tousled dark hair and several days' stubble. He was dressed in a one-piece black suit. His right eye was covered with a black eye-shield and he wore a triangular stud in his left ear.

Immigration control was a bare, metal area, bathed in harsh blue light. Humans and aliens shuffled forward in four queues. The visitor at the head of each queue waited for a green light, the signal for them to show their data-cards.

After 20 minutes, Caleb was second in line. In front of him was a Quaslon, a three-tusked creature in red robes. The Quaslon turned, gave Caleb a nod. It breathed out the red smoke that its race used as a greeting.

Caleb coughed, brushing the smoke away. 'Light's on, Tusky,' he snapped, nodding. The Quaslon, giving up on social niceties, shuffled forward.

'*Modify*,' said a mocking voice in Caleb's head. He shook his head. No. Not here. Not yet.

A few minutes later, it was Caleb's turn. He strode forward, slid his card into the reader on desk four. The officer, a young woman with a bald head and polished white skin, gave him a brisk smile.

'Good day, Citizen. Sorry for your wait.'

'Fine. I'm in no hurry.'

Tiny scan-drones buzzed around the metallic bag that was Caleb's only luggage. As the officer read his documents, her perfect eyebrows shot up a few centimetres.

'I see you have some… history, Citizen.'

Caleb scowled, folded his arms. 'Problem?'

'We'll see,' she said. Her twelve long, white fingers moved over her invisible keypad. 'Lift the tracker for me, please….'

Caleb sighed. He lifted the square of plastic, revealing his blank eye socket. 'Gonna ask me how I lost it?'

'Not interested,' she said, scanning his face with a handheld device. 'Just checking for hidden weaponry…. All right. You can put it down.'

'I heard Station Zero didn't ask questions,' Caleb said. He snapped the eye-shield back on.

She glanced up at him briefly. 'We stick to the essentials.' Caleb's data-card popped back out of the reader. 'Well, all seems to be in order.'

'Good,' said Caleb. The drones scattered, allowing him to pick his luggage up. 'Have a nice day.'

'*Modify!*' said the voice in his mind again, and once again he shook it off angrily.

Beyond the barrier, a woman in a crisp, white uniform was waiting. Her hair was grey and glossy, her dark skin smooth. She had high cheekbones and wore green glasses. Two burly male officers with rifles stood behind her.

The woman waved a hand. 'Just step over here, Citizen, would you?'

'I've... seen the girl,' Caleb said, waving a hand behind him.

'Yes,' said the woman, 'but you haven't seen *me*.' The ID plaque on her hand came to life, showing her face and badge number. 'Chief Alesha Quine. I head up the Security Force here. I know about you, Citizen Caleb Grayden.'

Her use of his name came as a shock. He tried not to let it show. 'OK… so what do you want, Chief? My autograph?'

'Just a friendly warning,' said Quine. She grinned, showing a set of perfect white teeth.

Now Caleb was up close, his tracker saw the pinpricks of regen-tissue on Quine's skin. To the naked eye, Quine was a woman of about 40. Caleb, though, guessed she was actually nearer 70 and on her fourth or fifth boost.

'I know who you are,' Quine continued, 'and *what* you are.'

Caleb shrugged, grinned lazily. 'Hey, it's neutral space. I keep my nose clean, you don't shove me out of an airlock. Works for me, works for you, Alesha. Can I call you Alesha?'

'No, you may not,' said Quine coldly. 'All right, Citizen. Go about your business. I think we'll speak again.'

Caleb gave her a mock salute. 'Sure thing, Chief,' he said, and he blew her a kiss as he moved through, bag hoisted on his shoulder.

Seconds later, he had joined the crowds in arrivals.

The hall was a vast arena. It was hot, noisy, and full of aliens of all shapes and sizes. There were green-skinned Balovians, scaly blue Warghis and humans of all races and types. The station staff were easy to spot in their crisp, white uniforms. At least twenty travel-tubes led off to the rest of the station.

Steam rose from the milling crowds. Coloured lights played on the various stalls, shops, social areas and bars. The noise of chattering, shouting, laughing and squealing – a thousand languages and dialects – filled the air. So did the pungent smells of alien bodies, of cooking meat, of alcohol and smoking plants. Caleb had travelled a lot in his work, but he'd never seen so many different beings in one place. He looked around, taking it all in.

He was dying to modify now. The urge was so strong.

'All right, babe. Your turn for a bit.'

He ducked into an alcove behind a booth piled high with trinkets and junk. The stallholder barely glanced at him.

It only took two seconds. His body seemed to shimmer. Dark hair fell to his shoulders, his chest and legs became shapely, and the dark suit became a slim-fitting dress and boots. The shield over her right eye was still in place, as was the ear stud, and the hair was of the same jet-black hue. Otherwise, this was a totally different person.

Caleb had given way to Keara.

She looked both ways. She was hoping nobody had seen her. She hoisted the sparkling bag onto her shoulder and stepped out into the crowd again with a confident smile.

*

In the shadows, the hidden watcher turned up the collar of a long, blue coat.

So, the watcher thought, a shifter. Here, on Zero. These people weren't good news. Radioactive mutants, hated in some parts of the galaxy. Under a kill order on many planets.

It was time to find out what this one really wanted.

CHAPTER 2
A FRIENDLY DRINK

'Hyperian Scotch. Double, with nitro-ice.'
Keara smiled at the barman, a Galactic Rim
native covered in tattoos of Earthling comic
strips. He nodded and mixed the drink quickly
with his four hands.

'I'm sorry,' said a breathy voice beside her. 'I saw
your... um... shift? I didn't mean to....'

Keara turned, eyes narrowed.

The new arrival was a plump young woman
dressed in a long, blue velvet coat, smart blue suit
and tie. She had blue hair to match, thick rimless

glasses and blue facial jewellery. She looked Earth-born. She was Euro-Asian, at a guess.

The girl caught the bartender's eye. 'Martian Spritzer, please.'

'Lucky for you I'm not shy,' said Keara. 'You want something?'

'No, I….' The young woman sighed. 'OK. Look. I'm Jandri Jax.' She offered her hand.

Keara shook her hand, unwillingly. 'Keara Grayden,' she said. 'And what do you do here?'

'Junior Legator. I'm just in my first year.'

'A lawyer?' Keara laughed. 'Touting for business, are you? Well, I haven't done anything wrong. Recently.' She sipped her whisky. 'Oh, and it's modify, if you don't mind. *Shift* is so Old Earth.'

'Sorry.' Jandri Jax held her hands up. 'Modify. Yes… so, you're the… secondary aspect? Is that right?'

Keara gulped her whisky, enjoying the burning sensation. 'Nosy, aren't you? Yeah, I'm the secondary. Caleb's my primary. He's not nice. Carry on pestering me and I'll modify back into him.' She blew a cloud of nitro-ice vapour, shuddering as it scalded her lips.

'How does it… *work*?' asked Jandri cautiously. Her Martian Spritzer, steaming and bubbling, arrived in a tall glass. She nodded her thanks and sipped it. 'I mean, are you, like… two different people?'

Keara gave her a weary look. She was so fed up with answering this question. Seriously, why? BMHs – binary modifying humanoids, or 'shifters' – had been around for centuries, and yet some people still didn't get it.

'Yes,' she said curtly. 'We have our own minds and our own opinions. Our bodies are different, but some aspects are the same. The same heart, for example. And if one of us is damaged…' She gestured to the eye-shield. 'We both take the hit.

And when one of us dies, we both die.'

'Sorry, I'm not being rude.' Jandri sipped her drink. 'I just like to understand.'

'You are being a bit rude,' said Keara, but she regretted it.

Jandri recoiled. 'Citizen, I didn't mean any offence. I just thought you might like a friend in this back-of-beyond place.'

'I don't really do *friends*,' said Keara, coldly.

Jandri leaned in to Keara, frowning. 'All right. It's just that… out here on the Rim… you may find people less understanding about shifters that they are in Galactic Centre.'

Keara gave her a look of disgust, then finished her whisky in one go. 'I don't want *understanding*,' she said. 'Caleb's here to do a job, and to hide away from a few people in Central. I'm just here for the ride.'

'I see.' Jandri peered over her glasses. 'What line of work is he in?'

Keara didn't answer.

'People rarely come here by choice,' said Jandri with a smile. 'This is a refuge, a hub for all the galaxy's trash. It's full of losers, wanderers, schemers and villains.'

Keara sneered. 'Poetically put. Feel at home, do you?'

Jandri grinned. 'I pick up a lot of work.' She slid her card along the bar. 'I'm pretty good, you know. I've won every case so far.'

Keara reached out to push the card back along the bar. Then something made her nod and take it.

Jandri smiled. 'You know where I am if you need me. Or Caleb does.'

Keara read the stencilled blue letters on the white background:

J.E.P. JAX, LEGATOR, RANK 1
- EARTH & GALACTIC.

Keara slipped the card into her bag. 'Thank you,' she said. 'Now will you go away?'

*

After a few hours of searching, Keara found a small room on Seventh Boulevard, in a dodgy area of Zero.

It was like one of the worst towns of Old Earth, she thought – full of drug dealers, prostitutes and beggars. The landlord, a leering Warghi with broken teeth, charged her twice as much as he should have done. She paid it, just to have somewhere to sleep.

Lying on the bed, she modified again with a very quick shimmer.

Caleb straightened up, stretching, easing the crick in his neck. It took a few minutes to settle comfortably back into the body each time. He was five centimetres taller than Keara, for one thing.

He stood at the window, looking out across the lights of Station Zero. It could have been one of Earth's old cities at night, he thought, with its clusters of domes and skyscrapers, and its twinkling streetlights. More than a million people were on this station at any one time, he knew. The biggest cluster of life outside the solar system.

He didn't like people much. He was keen to get the job done and get away.

As if reading his mind, the comlink on his bedside table buzzed. He stabbed at the button. There was no visual, just a spinning cone of purple light, and a voice.

'Caleb Grayden?' the voice asked.

'Who wants to know?' It was his usual guarded answer.

'The hit has just come on board Zero. Be in the Sky Park for further instructions at 0730 hours tomorrow morning.'

The cone of light rushed back into the comlink like water into a funnel, and the voice snapped off.

CHAPTER 3
THE HIT

At the agreed time, Caleb found himself alone in the Sky Park.

It was a beautiful, green space on a floating platform, dotted with marble sculptures and sparkling silver fountains. Fake sunlight glittered on a glassy lake. There were even a few ducks quacking. Caleb assumed they were robots, although they could have been real. A scent of jasmine carried on the artificial breeze, and there was a soft, warm feel to the morning air.

Caleb got comfortable on a bench and waited.

Above him, in the sky, the other side of Station Zero curved away from him. He could see the city waking, hear the hum of the morning traffic. He had to admit, Station Zero was a great feat of engineering. The fake gravity, the city, the way they controlled the lighting – all very impressive. Sitting there in the Sky Park, he could almost think he was out in the open air. He could have been in one of the Clean Areas on Earth, or on one of the terraformed colony worlds.

There was nobody else to be seen, apart from an athletic young man jogging, doing laps of the lake. The only sounds were the distant hum of the electric trains and the gentle splash of the fountain. Caleb checked his watch – 0729. He hoped his contact was going to be punctual.

He watched the jogger carefully.

Caleb smiled. He was pretty sure he had spotted his contact.

The jogger came around the lake at a fast pace. As he passed by, Caleb held his breath. Nothing.

Caleb frowned, staring after the jogger. He didn't like to be wrong.

'Beautiful morning.'

Caleb jumped. A figure had appeared silently on the bench beside him. Tall, black, athletic, wearing green sunglasses, a cool linen suit and a fedora. It was Chief Alesha Quine.

'How did you do that?' Caleb asked in admiration. He'd been distracted by the jogger. He told himself to be more alert.

'Training.' Quine, one hand draped casually over the back of the seat, didn't look at him. 'My fifty years in the Force.'

Caleb leaned back. 'So. The job comes from you, Chief? I should have guessed.'

'It's very easy. You keep it quick, and discreet.'

'Trust me. It's what I always do. And payment?'

'Half before, half on completion. I think that's how you usually work?'

Caleb smiled. 'You know me well.'

Alesha Quine nodded. 'Of course. Details are being downloaded to your comlink. Wait ten seconds, then look at it very casually.'

Caleb obeyed. The flat black screen of the comlink showed an ugly man in his fifties, with bushy eyebrows and jowls. Caleb felt a jolt of fear and excitement.

'Scorbius Vander?' he said. 'Here, on Station Zero?'

'He came in yesterday,' said Quine softly. 'We have some idea of what he's planning. It's not good.'

Caleb whistled. 'The guy's the worst child trafficker in the galaxies. Everyone knows that. And yet you've never been able to pin a thing on him.'

'Vander is part of a wider network, we're pretty sure. If we arrest and charge him, there are… complications. However… if we *remove* him….'

Caleb let silence hang in the air for a moment or two.

Quine glanced at him. 'You won't hesitate?'

'Your own people could do this,' Caleb argued.

Quine laughed. 'Be serious. The Security Force can't be seen to be involved.'

'I see. Won't soil your lily-white hands, but happy to hire the job out.'

'Look. I know your story, Caleb. Being an assassin's a way of life for you. But everyone you've killed….' She left the sentence incomplete, but Caleb finished it for her.

'They've all deserved it,' he said. 'Murderers, torturers, serial rapists… people who wouldn't have been brought to justice.'

Annoyed that she'd missed the report, Jandri held her comlink up to download and catch up with the live broadcast. Then she hurried to the platforms and caught her train just as it was about to leave. She found her usual seat in the sleek silver bullet of the train. She put a privacy field up and flicked the report on to her personal screen.

'Station Zero Network is getting reports of a disturbance in Galaxia Plaza. We believe shots have been fired. Security Force tells us that a man aged 56-EY has been killed. They believe him to be the criminal Scorbius Vander, who is wanted for crimes of child exploitation, trafficking and assault in seven galaxies. The shooter is currently unknown. It is believed that he may have used a pixelation filter to hide himself from the CCTV cameras.'

Jandri peered forward interestedly as sloweddown, close-up footage of a scuffle appeared on the screen, flipped into 3D for the viewers.

The camera – probably a drone, she realised – hovered over the little knot of people. Jandri peered closely at the screen, pausing the image so she could see it more clearly. She flicked it with her fingertips, turning it round and round to view it from all angles. There was a burly man in a thick, dark coat, caught in mid-stride. She could see enough of the jowls and bushy eyebrows to be sure that this was indeed the deadly criminal Scorbius Vander, with two of his henchmen.

Jandri had heard of him, of course – all legators had. Some of her colleagues dreamed of bringing him to trial and prosecuting him. Some of them even dreamed of defending him, just for the challenge.

Jandri slowly sped the image up and watched what happened. A blurry, fast-moving figure passed Vander in the crowded square. It seemed to touch his arm. The henchmen could not move fast enough, but they whirled around and tried to fire plasma-shots after the dark figure. People in the square were screaming, dropping to the floor, pulling each other down.

Something flashed on to Jandri's screen as her train hurtled into the tunnel. A red disc saying 'LATEST UPDATE'. She patched the audio back in.

'It's understood that two citizens are being treated in hospital for minor injuries following the incident earlier today in Galaxia Plaza, in which one person was killed. Security has reassured all citizens that it is safe to go about their business. Station Zero's level of alert remains at green.'

'*That*,' thought Jandri Jax, '*sounds as if they know more than they're letting on.*'

The train pulled into her station. She snapped the comlink shut and hurried to the doors.

*

'The 2330 departure for Sol Central,' said Caleb.

He looked nervously over his shoulder as he presented his boarding pass to the clerk. The departure hall was busy. He had wasted no time in booking the earliest flight out. Half the money was, as agreed, already in his account. He was waiting for the rest.

The clerk nodded. He took Caleb's pass and scanned it.

There was a low beeping noise, and a red light flashed on the desk. The clerk frowned.

'I'm sorry, Mr Grayden,' he said. 'There seems to be a block on this pass.'

'A block?' said Caleb, puzzled. 'What does that mean?'

A hand came down on his shoulder, turned him around with some force. He was looking into the eyes of Alesha Quine.

She smiled, peering over her green glasses. Behind her stood three armed officers in crisp, white uniforms, helmets and visors. They were all levelling their guns at Caleb.

'It means,' said Alesha Quine softly, 'that you, Caleb Grayden, are under arrest for the murder of Citizen Scorbius Vander.'

For once in his life, Caleb was lost for words.

CHAPTER 4
DEATH SENTENCE

He sat in a bare, steel-walled cell.

He'd been there an hour, so he had already checked out the escape potential. There was none. His plan had involved breaking the light panel and using the edge of the glass as a weapon, but that would mean being able to stand to reach it. And right now, his ankles were clamped to the chair.

He tried modifying to wriggle free, but the clamps self-adjusted. Keara's slimmer ankles were held just as firmly.

Frustrated, he modified back again.

*

They had given him a plastic jug of water and a beaker, and that was it.

He was pretty sure all of this was against all Station Zero regulations. He was also pretty sure Quine didn't care about that.

The door slid silently open and Quine came in. She was followed by a blond-haired man with a goatee beard, dressed in a dark, high-collared suit. Quine smiled and nodded at Caleb as if they were old friends.

'Citizen Grayden. I hope you are finding the accommodation comfortable?'

'Oh, I've had worse,' he said, and he wasn't lying. 'Who's your friend?'

The bearded man, sorting through some papers, looked up and smiled. 'Prosecutor Seb Chaney,' he said with a nod. 'At your service. I'm looking forward to making sure you serve the appropriate sentence for this crime.'

Caleb was struggling to get his head around the way the law worked on Station Zero. It was bad enough that the Chief had hired him to do a hit in the morning and then arrested him for it that same evening. But meeting his prosecutor before he even ended up in court? Before he had even officially been charged or interviewed? That was insane.

He was almost nostalgic for the way they did things back on Earth. The officials there were inept and stupid and would sometimes beat you up for fun, but at least they usually got things in the right order.

'I hope you've got a good case, Prosecutor. What's your evidence?'

Prosecutor Chaney looked at Alesha Quine, who nodded. 'All the evidence we need,' he said.

Alesha Quine held up a clear plastic wallet with a small red disc inside. 'Know what this is?' she asked, pointing to the disc.

'You tell me,' Caleb said, although he knew.

'A shocker. Causes a rather nasty death. Mixes up the atoms in the body and paralyses the victim in seconds. They usually die in under a minute. Your usual method, I think.' She sat back. 'Prosecutor?'

Chaney swept his hand across the table. Pictures sprang into life on its surface, clear holo-images of the murder of Scorbius Vander. Caleb could tell straightaway that they had been mocked up by computer – no way was the drone footage that clear.

The first showed Caleb, his face half hidden by a hood, reaching out to Vander's hand as they passed in the crowd. The next showed him with the red disc in his hand, placing it on Vander's neck. The one after that showed Vander dropping to the ground, his henchmen drawing their guns and firing after Caleb.

'So? These are all fakes,' said Caleb with a shrug.

Alesha Quine pressed her fingers together, swivelling back and forth on her chair. 'What makes you so sure of that?'

He smiled. 'Trust me,' he said. 'I know.'

'Accusing the authorities of faking evidence? You're on dangerous ground, Citizen.'

He shrugged. 'Yeah, but I'm right. I know.'

'You'd only know,' sneered Quine, 'if you were there.'

'What about you, Prosecutor?' Caleb said. 'Are you buying this crap? She's *fitted me up*, as they used to say on Old Earth.'

'Oh, come now,' said Alesha Quine, and tutted. 'Is that the best you can do, Citizen Grayden?'

Prosecutor Chaney's eyes were sharp, blue and piercing as he spoke. 'You know the law here, Citizen. You are guilty unless proven innocent. And the penalty for murder is death.' He smiled grimly. 'Got yourself a good lawyer?'

Caleb's heart sank. He knew nobody here on Zero. He was well and truly in trouble.

And then he remembered.

His face broke into a broad grin.

A voice in his head said: *'I'm pretty good, you know. I've won every case so far.'*

'Actually,' said Caleb, 'I have. And I'd like to call her, please.'

*

After Jandri Jax got Caleb's call, she spent all of the next two days going over and over the evidence.

She was desperate to win this case. As a Junior Legator, to win a case of this nature could push her career on to the next level. Jandri was nothing if not ambitious, and she knew an opportunity when she saw one.

For those two days, she hardly slept. She tried Bangraxian coffee, triple the strength of Earth's, but that just gave her the shakes. On the second night, she found herself falling asleep at her desk. She was going over the CCTV of Vander's murder frame by frame to see if there was anything she had missed.

Then something made her sit up, peering through her thick glasses.

'Wait a second,' she said. 'Pause image.'

Jandri's heart pounded with excitement. It wasn't just the Bangraxian coffee. She had found something.

Her excellent memory called up the name of someone she had been at university with. Within seconds the database had his current location – Olympus City on Mars. Jandri put in a sub-light call, drumming her fingers as it connected.

'Hello?' said a sleepy voice.

'Hi, is that Marcus Zane?'

'Who wants to know?' said the voice in irritation.

'Marcus, it's Jandri Jax. You remember? We were at New World together, back in '32.'

There was a moment's pause. Then, 'Jandri… Jandri Jax! What the hell…? I mean… great to hear from you!'

She did not have time to waste on social chit-chat. 'Sorry, Marc, I know I woke you up, but… I was wondering if I could pick your brains.'

'Sure. Glad to help if I can.'

She took a deep breath. 'Do you know anything about pixelation filters? And more to the point… how to get past them?'

CHAPTER 5
JUSTICE SERVED?

'OK,' said Jandri to Caleb, 'we're on.'

In his cell, Caleb straightened up.

Speed had been necessary. Two days was all
they had, under the law of the Galactic Rim,
to put together a case. Otherwise Caleb was
automatically found guilty, and would be
executed. He understood an atom chamber was
their way of doing it. It was quick and painless,
but that didn't reassure him.

'We need to win this,' he said to Jandri Jax.

She smiled. 'Afraid of death, Mr Assassin?'

'Not afraid, especially. I just haven't booked in for it yet. I rather wanted to see Andromeda before I die. How about you?'

'Yeah,' she said. 'I'd love to go to Andromeda.'

Caleb grinned. 'Maybe we could go together.'

Jandri raised a finger, mock sternly. 'Behave. Now, remember. Let me do all the talking. Chaney's already given them his evidence, so there's nothing we can do there.'

'What, didn't we get to hear it?' Caleb was confused. 'Don't you get to ask questions and so on?' He had a vague memory of Old Earth viscasts, of men in wigs and robes standing and loudly saying, 'Objection!'

Jandri smirked, as if she knew what he was thinking of. 'Don't you believe it. They have their own way of doing things here on the Rim. Convention says we present our evidence

separately. On one of these.' She held up a
sparkling, purple data-crystal. 'Shall we go?'

*

A floating platform took them up through
the darkness to the glowing pyramid of the
Justice Hall.

'It's obvious what Quine wants,' said Jandri Jax.
'You and Vander – two birds with one stone.
Both out of the way.'

Keara smiled. 'Yeah, well. This bird's not
dead yet.'

Jandri did a double take. She hadn't even noticed
her client modifying – she had left the holding
cells with Caleb. 'You need to modify back. It's
part of my case.'

Shrugging, Keara obeyed. She shimmered back
into Caleb.

The platform arrived in a vast, dark space, lit only by the orange globes in which the three Justicians sat. Noble, wise, impossibly old, they heard every case on Station Zero. A smaller, blue globe floated in front of them.

Prosecutor Chaney was there, smug and happy as he was escorted out. The prosecution evidence had obviously gone down well. Alesha Quine and her team were looking down from the observers' gallery. The clerk, a small, blue-skinned humanoid, was waiting there, too, hands behind her back.

The globes glowed as the Justicians greeted Jandri Jax and her client.

'Learned Legator Jax,' said the First Justician, in the central globe. He leaned forward, a hint of wizened skin visible under the cowled hood. 'You have summarised your evidence?'

'Yes, Your Honour.'

'Then bring it forward!'

Jandri Jax bowed. She stepped forward into the light, and brought the crystal to the clerk. He inserted it into the blue globe in front of the justicians. The globe flared bright blue for a second.

'The evidence will be analysed,' said the First Justician gravely. 'You will hear a verdict in two hours.'

The globes dimmed and began to retreat.

Jandri Jax steeled herself, and stepped forward into the spotlight again. She knew that she was taking a risk, but it had to be done. 'Your Honours, may I speak?'

For a few seconds, there was a tense silence in the Justice Hall. Then the globes flared with light again, and the First Justician's voice boomed out.

'What is it? Speak.'

'Your Honours,' said Jandri Jax carefully, 'the penalty for murder on Station Zero is death. In many other parts of the galaxy, the death penalty was abolished years ago. People have moved on to more... humane methods of justice, and – '

'Learned Legator, you are not here to take issue with the law,' said the First Justician testily. 'That is a matter for the Galactic Government.'

'Yes... yes, Your Honours, I know, but... please allow me to make my point.' Jandri Jax knew she was on shaky ground. 'You see, my client is... rather special. Caleb?'

She nodded to him, and in an instant he realised what she wanted him to do. With a shrug of his shoulders he modified, and Keara, her hair in a neat bun, stood there in the light.

There was silence from the Justicians.

'My problem is,' said Jandri, 'that if you find my client, Caleb Grayden, guilty and execute him, you also execute Keara, who is not guilty, and, indeed, is not charged with any crime. You see the issue.'

The Justicians' globes huddled together as they conferred, orange lights flickering in the darkness. Jandri shot a triumphant look up at Alesha Quine.

Quine narrowed her eyes.

Despite her confidence, Jandri Jax was still not entirely certain that she was going to get away with this.

CHAPTER 6
PROFESSIONAL PRIDE

Two hours later, it was all over.

A relieved Caleb clinked glasses with Jandri Jax in the 54th-floor cocktail bar of the Station Zero's Trillennium Tower. The whole station was spread out before them like glittering dust.

'I must confess,' said Jandri, 'I didn't think they'd go for it.'

'Nor did I!' said Caleb in admiration. 'Deferred banishment. Great result. It's the best I could have hoped for.'

Jandri narrowed her eyes at him through her little round glasses. 'You're a dark horse, aren't you? Both of you.'

'What do you mean?'

'Oh, just a little thing I discovered when looking at the evidence. It doesn't make any difference to the verdict, though.'

Caleb stared at her, curiously. Something clicked in his brain. He suddenly realised what Jandri meant.

Jandri glanced at her watch. 'And now I mention it – three hours, the Justicians gave you. About time you were getting out of here.'

Caleb hoisted his bag on to his shoulder, smiling ruefully at the lights of Station Zero.

Little did Jandri know, but there was one more job to be done before he left for good.

*

In the elevator, soft orange light played over them both as they descended. Caleb modified silently into Keara. Jandri was checking messages on her comlink.

'I do appreciate all your work,' said Keara. 'And so does Caleb. You were very cunning. You played the system.'

Jandri Jax barely glanced up from her comlink. 'All part of the job,' she said, with a wave of her hand.

'I imagine this'll be great for your career.'

The young legator grinned. 'I hope so.'

'You know,' said Keara softly, 'one thing never changes in this universe.'

'Mm?' said Jandri, looking up. 'What's that?'

'Somewhere,' she said, turning slowly to look at Jandri, 'there's always a man ready to take the credit for a woman's work. In this case, though, it suits both Caleb and me for that to be the case.'

There was silence in the elevator as it continued to descend the 500 floors to the Spaceport.

'Ah,' said Jandri Jax awkwardly. 'You know.'

'Yes,' said Keara with a smile. 'And I'm impressed.'

'Impressed?'

'That you worked it out. I thought my pixelation filter was faultless. How did you manage to see through it?'

Jandri smirked. 'Well, I had the help of an old friend on Mars who knows one or two things about tech wizardry. It wasn't that hard. I sent him the v-file, and he sent it back unscrambled within the hour.'

'And you saw,' said Keara, 'what we've managed to keep hidden for years. Very clever.'

'It's not a bad trick,' said Jandri. She smiled. 'Caleb gets the reputation as the fearless assassin, and nobody ever suspects the secondary aspect. The real killer. Got to admit – it's clever.'

'I'm afraid it is,' said Keara sadly. 'And nobody can ever know.'

The elevator continued to descend.

*

Five hours later, Security Team Delta managed to clear the jammed elevator-tube in the Trillennium Tower.

The officer in charge had to report that, inside the elevator pod, they found the body of a female, aged approximately 25-EY. She was identified as a Junior Legator, Jandri Eliza Persephone Jax.

On her cold forehead, like a calling card, was the small red disc of a shocker.

Security Chief Alesha Quine, on hearing that news, sank back into her chair with her mouth set grimly, eyes narrowed. She knew she could put out an all points recall, but it would be worthless. By now, the killer would be light years away from Station Zero.

And she was never coming back.

ABOUT THE AUTHOR

Daniel Blythe is the author of more than 20 books, including several of the *Doctor Who* novels, as well as *Shadow Runners* and *Emerald Greene and the Witch Stones*. He is originally from Maidstone, but now lives with his wife and two teenage children in Yorkshire. He has been published in 12 countries including the USA, Germany and Brazil, and he has led writing days and workshops in more than 400 schools.